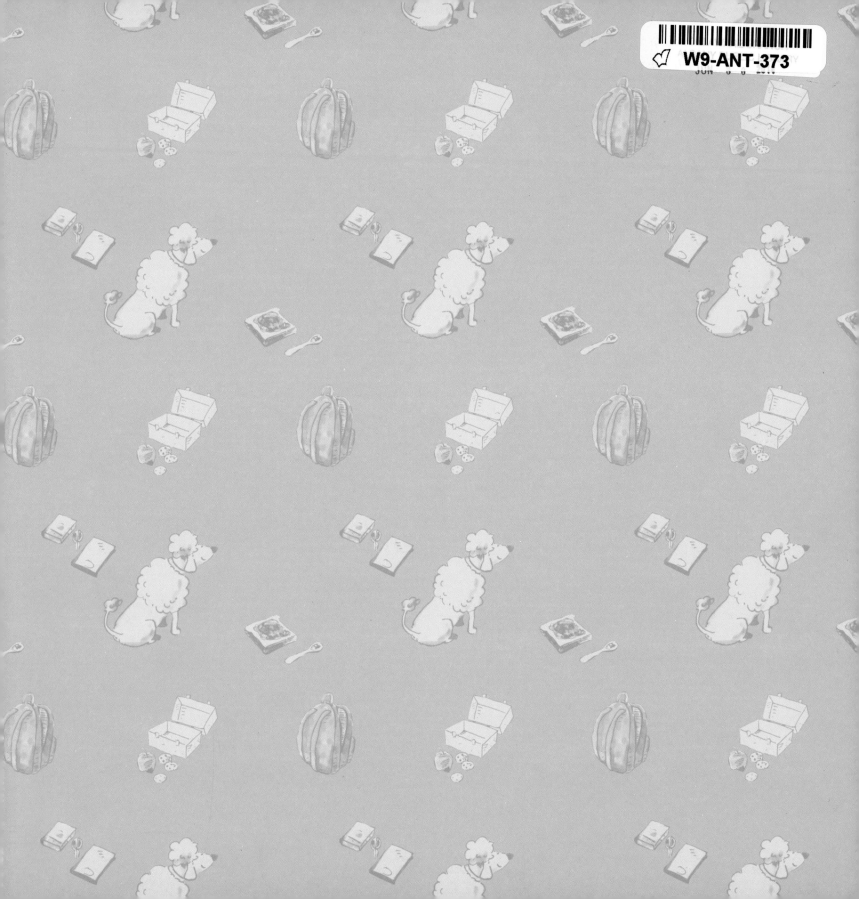

The Night Before First Grade

By Natasha Wing

Illustrated by Deborah Zemke

Grosset & Dunlap
An Imprint of Penguin Group (USA) LLC

To best friends—NW
Thank you, Mrs. Greene—DZ

The Library of Congress has cataloged the paperback edition under the following Control Number: 2004017865

ISBN 978-0-448-48256-9   10 9 8 7 6 5 4 3 2 1

BEST FRIENDS

'Twas the night before first grade.
I kissed my dog, Clover.
"School's starting tomorrow
because summer is over."

Into my backpack
went markers and pens.

I hung my new outfit—
it matched my friend Jen's.

I spoke not a word
but went straight to the shelf
and filled up my lunchbox.
I made lunch myself!

"I can't wait to see Jenny!"
I told my big brother.
"I hope that our desks
are right next to each other."

That night, I was nestled all snug in my bed while visions of jungle gyms danced in my head.

The next day at breakfast,
Dad made such a fuss.
"What a big girl you are
to be taking the bus."

"Hurry, Penny," said Mom
as it turned down our street.
"Over here!" shouted Jenny.
"I saved you a seat."

At school, kindergartners
stood outside in the hall.
They all looked so young.
Were we ever that small?

While they clung to their parents,
we hugged Miss Sunrise.
"You two grew so tall!" she
said with surprise.

D-d-d-ding rang the school bell.
We made such a clatter as we raced to our classroom.

Then Jen said,
"What's the matter?"

The principal told us that some
changes were made.
"We have some new students.
So we split the first grade."

"Hi, Penny!" said my teacher.
"You're in here with me."
But—yipes!—Jenny wasn't!
She was in Room Thirty-Three.

We waved good-bye sadly
and said, "See you later."

I had to be brave
because I'm a first-grader.

Soon we sat in a circle.
And we each said our name.
Then we played twenty questions,
and **I** won the game!

Mr. Barr is so funny!
He tells jokes and he juggles.

And our class pet's so cute—
it's a bunny named Snuggles.

I knew most of the kids,
except just a few.
So I went and said hi
to a girl who was new.

We sat side by side
and made pictures with noodles.

We laughed when we saw
we both made noodle poodles.

We both have pet turtles
and love turquoise blue.
And pistachio ice cream
is her favorite, too.

"I can't wait till you meet
my best friend at lunch.
I just know that you'll both
like each other a bunch."

The lunchroom was buzzing—
so busy and loud!
We sat down at a table.
Was Jen in this crowd?

When what to my wondering
eyes—there in line—
was Jen with a new friend who
looked just like mine!

Their eyes—how they twinkled—
behind matching frames!
They had curly pigtails
and they had rhyming names!

Our new friends were twins,
and though school's just begun,
I know first grade will be
twice as much fun!

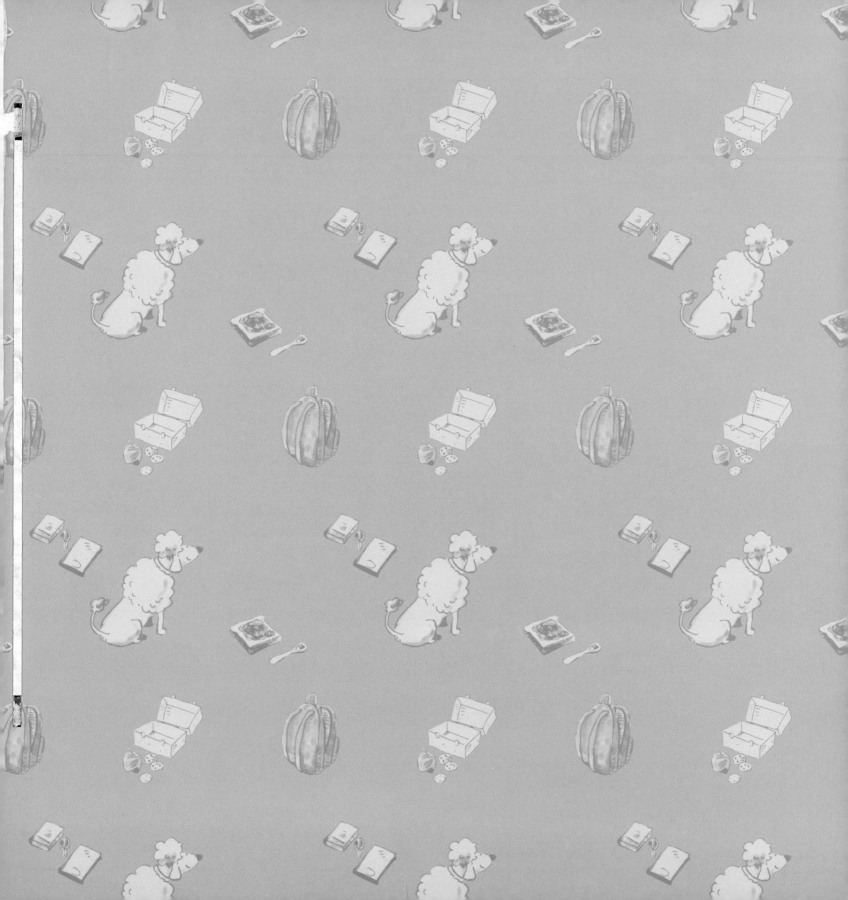

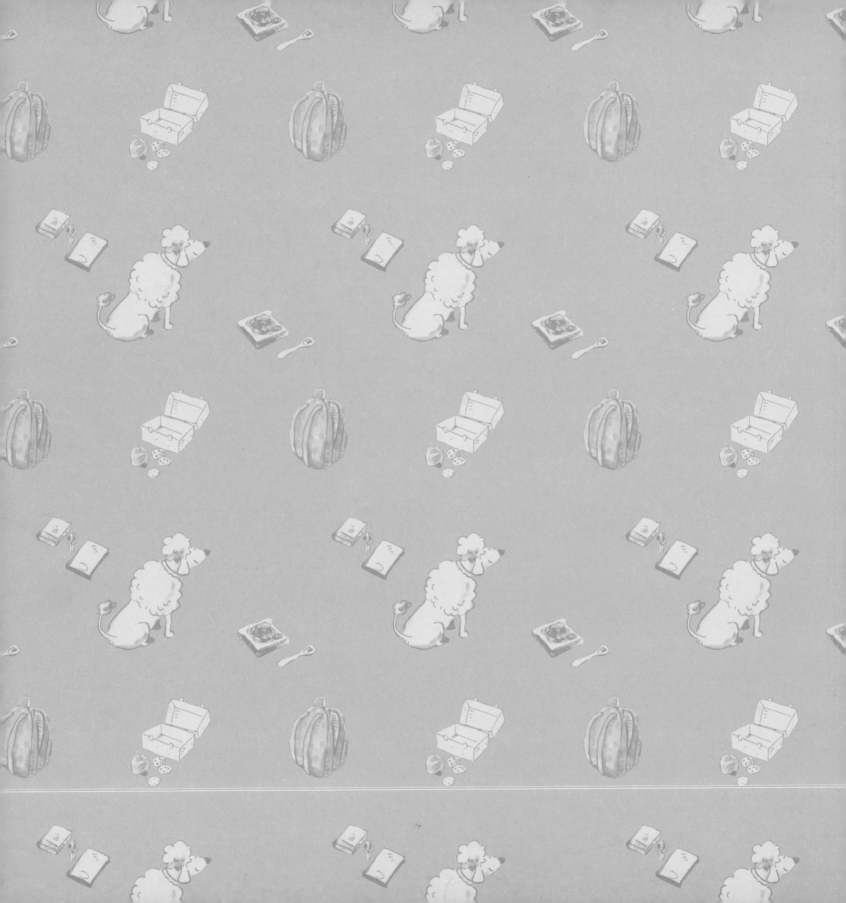